big & SMALL

Original Korean text by Mi-ae Lee
Illustrations by Hae-ryun Jeong
Korean edition © Dawoolim

This English edition published by Big & Small in 2015
by arrangement with Dawoolim
English text edited by Joy Cowley
English edition © Big & Small 2015

Distributed in the United States and Canada by
Lerner Publishing Group, Inc.
241 First Avenue North
Minneapolis, MN 55401 U.S. A.
www.lernerbooks.com

ISBN: 978-1-925186-19-2

Printed in the United States of America

Secrets of Air

Written by Mi-ae Lee
Illustrated by Hae-ryun Jeong
Edited by Joy Cowley

Air softly wraps the Earth
where we all live.

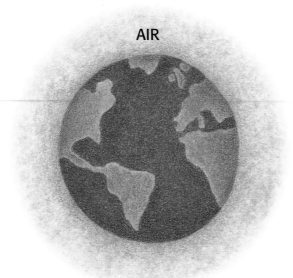

AIR

Because air wraps the Earth,
it is not too hot in the daytime
and not too cold at night.

Air is close to the earth,
above the pointed roof
and between the trees.

When we go to the top
of a high mountain,
there is less air
so it is harder to breathe.

Air moves swiftly over me
when I ride my bicycle.

It gusts when Granny fans me.
It flutters when I clap my hands.

We cannot see, smell or touch the air.
But we can feel air because when we move,
it moves too.

11

Wind is moving air.
When the wind blows,
grasses dance in the field
and leaves swirl around.
My hat blows away in the wind.

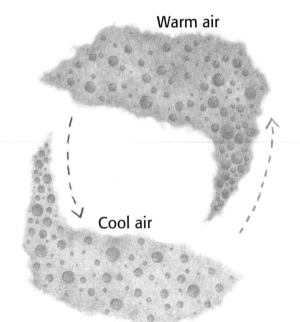

Warm air

Cool air

Warm air is light, so it goes up.
Cool air is heavy and goes down.
As air moves up and down,
wind is created.

My little windmill is spinning.
Wind pushes the sailboat
and flies the kite up high.

We can do anything with air.
When we put air in a rubber boat,
it floats on the water.

A storm brings wind and rain.
Waves are big.
Boats are tossed.

Warm air above the sea
creates hurricanes and typhoons.
It causes strong winds
and lots of rain.

16

Tweet, tweet!
Birds are chirping.
Buzz, buzz!
Insects are humming.
Without air,
we would not hear them.

Air carries sound waves
and passes sound to us.
When we close a door or window
we cannot hear the sound outside.

Air is very light
and not heavy to lift.
We can carry lots of balloons
that have been filled with air.

A plastic bottle full of air
is only as heavy as a bean.

When we breathe in,
air comes into our body.
When we breathe out,
air goes out of our body.

Oxygen   Carbon dioxide

When we breathe in
we use the oxygen in the air
and exhale carbon dioxide.

Air gets polluted and stuffy
with the smoke from cars
and the heat
from air conditioners.

When we breathe polluted air,
we may develop skin problems or a headache.
We should cover our mouth and nose
with a mask when we are in dusty places.

When grass and trees breathe out,
they let out oxygen
which cleans the air.
Trees need lots of sunlight
to manufacture the oxygen.

Oxygen

Plants produce nutrients by absorbing sunlight,
and oxygen is made during this process.
This is why we feel refreshed
when we are in a forest.

Air is precious and very important.
Let's try to keep our air clean.

There is no air on the moon.
That is why people wear spacesuits.

Secrets of Air

Air is everywhere but it is invisible and odorless.

Let's think

What is air made of?

How does wind happen?

How does air carry sound?

Why is polluted air bad?

Let's do!

Get an empty balloon and blow air into the balloon until it is full.

What happens when you let go of the balloon?

Where does the air in the balloon go?